# Brown Is Warm, Black Is Bright

Words by **Sarah L. Thomson**

Art by **Keith Mallett**

**L** **B**

**Little, Brown and Company**
New York  Boston

Brown is crisp...

crunch and crackle,
catch me as I fall.

*Black is splash...*

Spray! Splatter!
to send a puddle flying.

Brown is strong . . .

a ship to hold me
high in leafy seas.

Black is flight...

inky wings
on wet watercolor clouds.

*Brown is beckoning...*

a faithful path
to follow all the way home.

Black is hope…

floating far,
a flower hidden deep.

*Brown is sweet...*

a spoon of sunlight
swirling in my cup.

*Black is blossoming...*

ideas opening,
unfurling on a page.

*Brown is rich…*

a river of sound
rushing from rippling strings.

Black is bright...

tender darkness
glowing between stars.

Brown is safe...

when your hand
holds mine.

Black is deep...

when your eyes meet mine.

*Brown is warm...*

soft and breathing,
curled up next to me.

*Black is quiet...*

as a kiss…

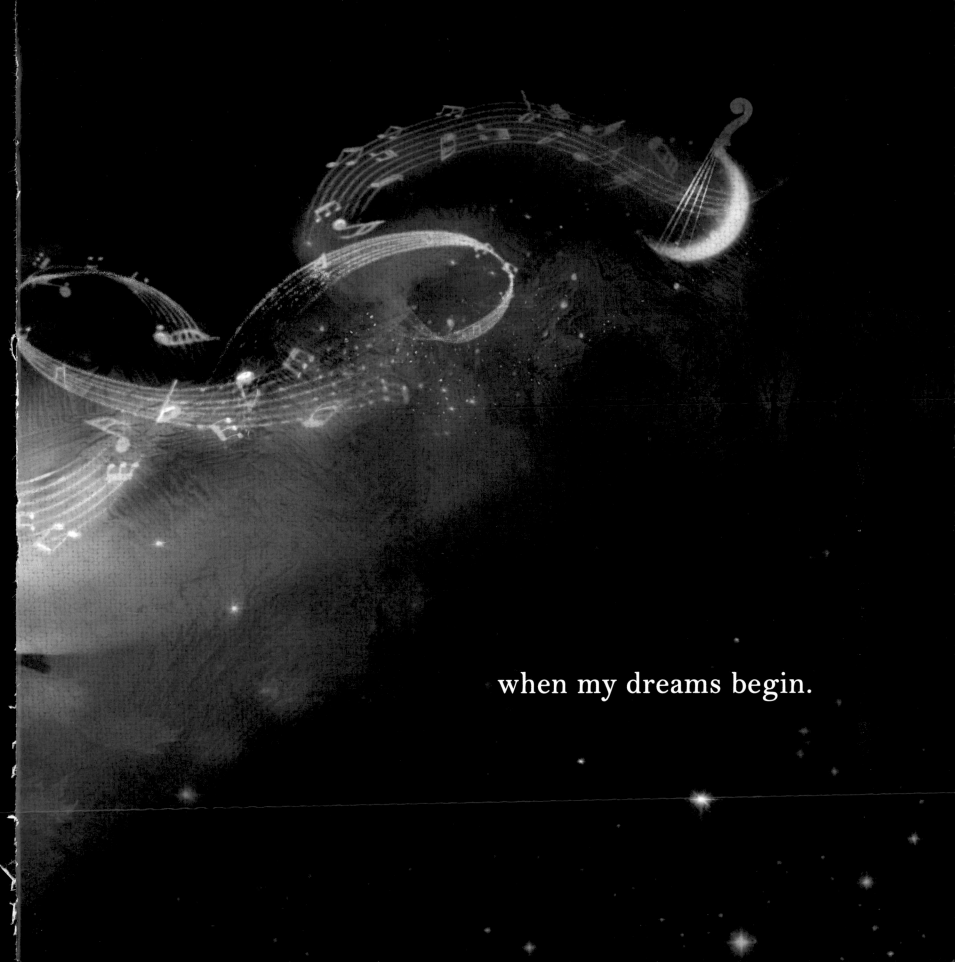

when my dreams begin.

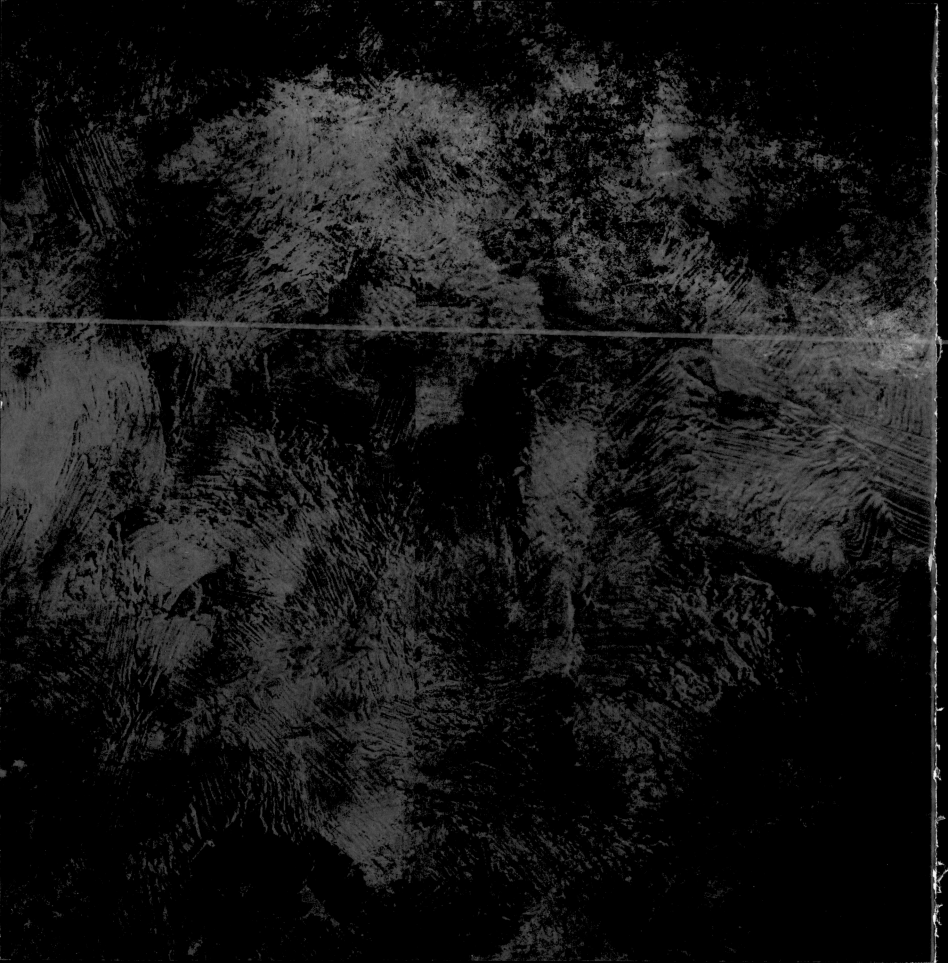